# The Crawling Hand

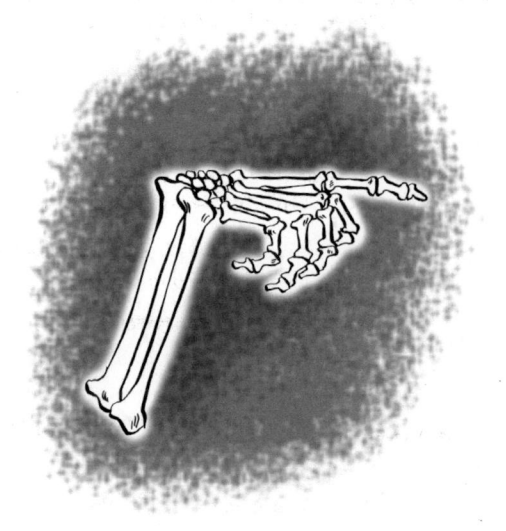

Andrew Fusek Peters
and Cathy Brett

# Freestylers

## Titles in the series

### The Crawling Hand
9780750268950

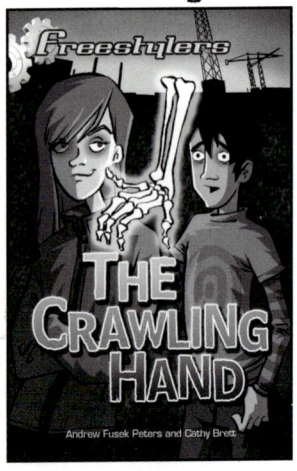

### Sliced in Two
9780750268967

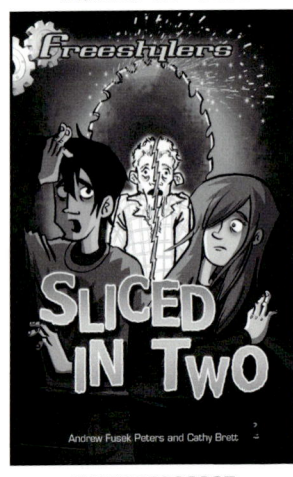

### Wolf Boy
9780750268974

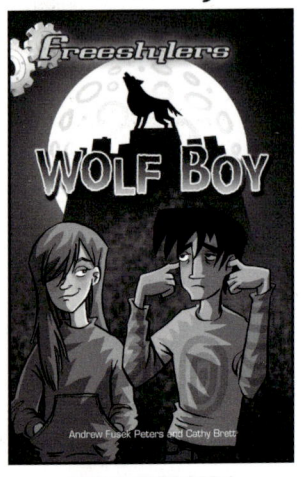

### High Stakes
9780750268981

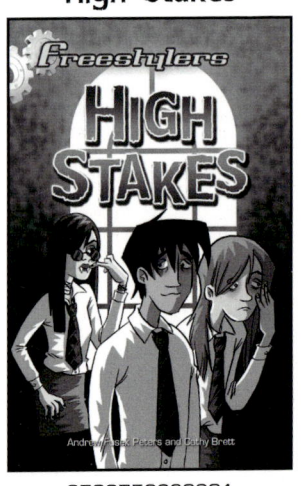

# THE CRAWLING HAND

## CHAPTER 1

I was hanging around with Sam when I first heard the sound. Skritch. Skritch. Skritch.

"What's that?" Sam cried. Her chewing gum dropped out of her mouth.

"Could be a tree?" I said.

"Jas, there aren't any trees near your mum's garage. For a detective, you can be quite stupid sometimes."

Oh yes. By the way, that's my name. Jas, short for Jasinder.

# THE CRAWLING HAND

One of the best detectives around. Lost dog? Mobile been nicked? I'm your man.

There it was again. Skritch. Skritch. Skritch. My chair was on rollers. I slid backwards to the shelves.

"We're going to die!" I yelped.

"What?" said Sam. "From a scratch?"

The sound stopped. The door handle turned in slow motion and the door screeched open.

# THE CRAWLING HAND

I gripped the arm of my chair, waiting for the worst.

"Good evening."

This was odd. There was nothing there. I've never had a

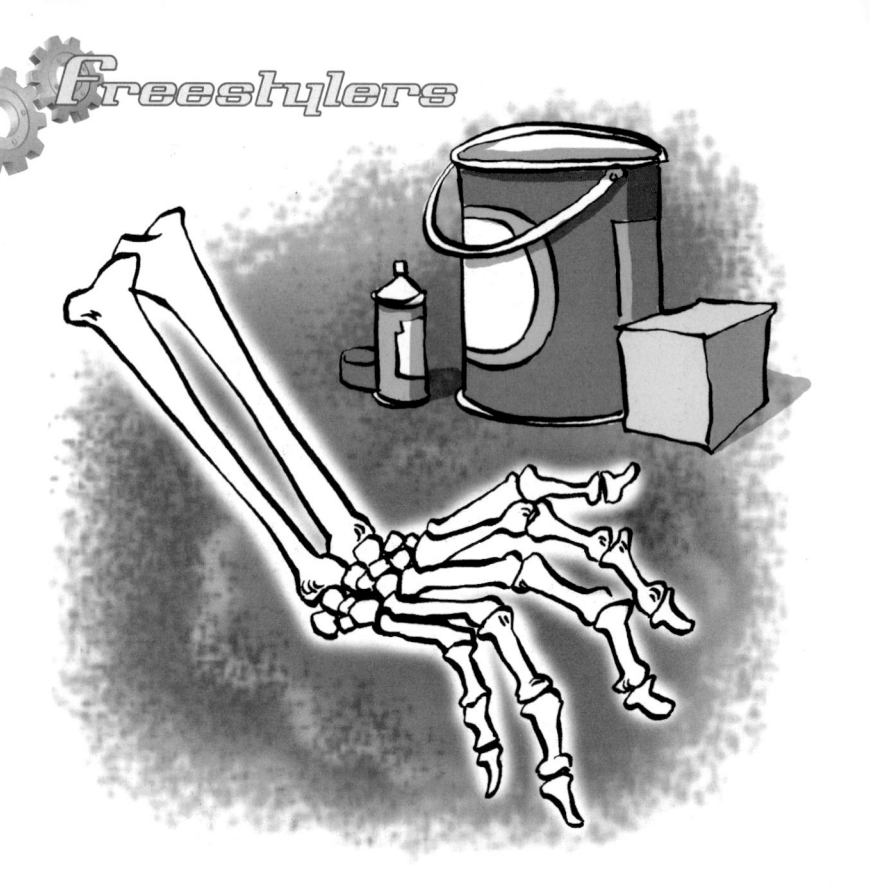

bit of nothing talk to
me before.

"Who's there?" I squeaked.

I looked down. It was a hand!
Well… the bones of a hand.
Right now, they were crawling

# THE CRAWLING HAND

over the dusty floor right towards us.

"Oh no!" Sam screeched, her eyeballs nearly popping out. "That's so gross!"

"I hope I'm not bothering

you, Jas and Sam." The voice was dry and crackly.

"Bothered? Me? Help me out here, Sam!"

Sam tried to stop her own hands shaking. "Yeah. We're not bothered by the sight of a walking, talking hand. But how can you talk without a mouth?"

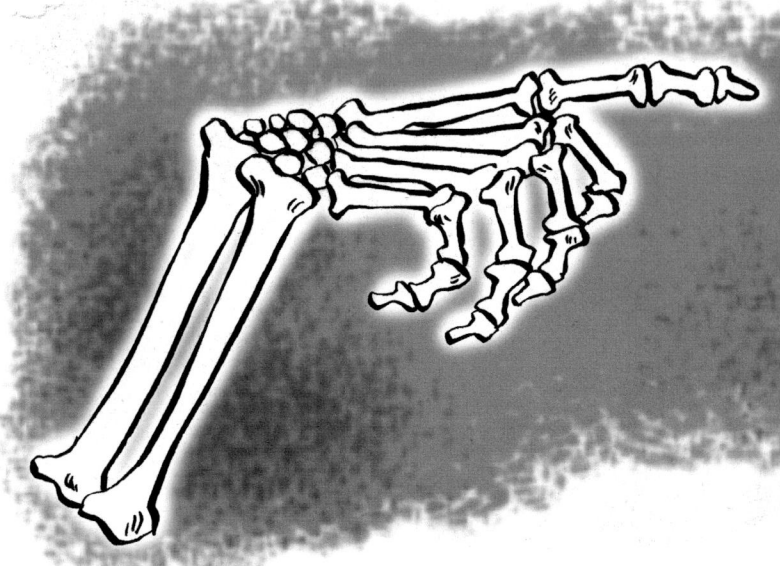

# THE CRAWLING HAND

"Never really thought about it," the hand went on.

"And how do you know our names?"

The hand crooked a bony finger and pointed at us.

"You have a reputation."

"We do?"

Despite shaking like a leaf, I couldn't help smiling.

"The point is, I've come to you about a missing body."

"You're missing a few more

# THE CRAWLING HAND

things than just a body!" said Sam. "Like skin, oh, and a bit of life, maybe?" She tried to sound cool but her voice was wobblier than a trifle.

"Yes, being dead isn't great, but someone has snatched my body!" The hand spun around in a circle on one finger, sticking its wrist into the air. "See? No body there!"

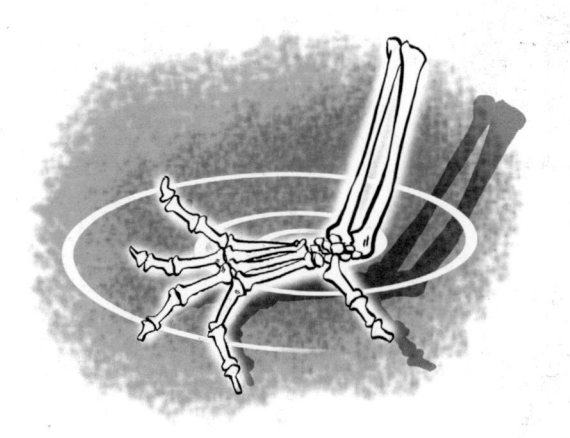

The sight of all that white bone made me feel sick.

"And you want us to help?"

"That's the idea."

Our detective motto is 'Be Prepared!' But, hey, it's not every day that something dead pops by for a chat.

## CHAPTER 2

"We'll be late for tea!"

"Oh, stop moaning, Jas. We'll never solve this case if you don't shut up!"

Sam was right as usual, even though I was starving. At least

she was carrying the hand.
The thought of it still made me
feel sick. "Where are we going?"

"Take a left after the park.
You'll see," said the hand.

# The Crawling Hand

Five minutes later we were there. "But this is a building site!" said Sam. At this time of night it was empty.

"No!" said the hand, perched like a bird on her palm. "This is my resting place."

# Freestylers

I looked at the notice on the wire fence. "Coming soon, a brand new Hoggins Supermarket. Only The Best!" There was a picture of Widow Hoggins smiling. Behind the fence there was a great big

# The Crawling Hand

hole in the ground.

"Listen, finger-face, you've got it all wrong!" I said. "This is just a bunch of mud and rubble!"

The bones began to clack together noisily.

"Listen to me," it wailed. "I was sleeping, nice and cosy

in my coffin when something big and shiny ripped the lid off and stole my body away."
A finger pointed onto the site. "One of those!"

There were three diggers lined up in a row.

# The Crawling Hand

"No way!" said Sam. "Body snatching. That's against the law!"

"Why would they steal a skeleton? It doesn't make any sense."

"It wasn't just me. All my friends, too."

I scratched my chin. "So, now we're looking for a gang of skeletons. Great."

"I've got it!" Sam said. "I read about it at school once. Old graveyards. You can't build on them."

# THE CRAWLING HAND

"Oh," I smiled. "So when the graves were dug up, the boss decided to keep it a secret?"

"Jas! You have a brain! Maybe you aren't so dumb after all!"

"Hey!" The shout was loud

enough to make us jump out of our skins. We turned and made a run for it as a man came sprinting towards us waving a huge spanner in his hand.

## CHAPTER 3

"That was close!" I whispered, as we hid behind a bush. It was wet, but at least it wasn't going to kill us.

"Too right," said Sam. "Are you okay, Hand?"

"You may call me Ron, after

my master," said the hand, "And yes, I still have all my bones. Thank you for asking."

"What do we do now?" I asked.

"It's very plain," said Sam, as

she crawled out of the bush.

"It is?" I said.

"Yes. If the boss is behind this, then she's the one who has hidden the bodies. All we have to do is find them."

"I knew that!" Sam was getting more annoying every day.

"Good. The street's clear. Let's go!"

I peered nervously through the leaves. "Are you sure it's

# THE CRAWLING HAND

safe out there?"

"Course I am! Now, how am I going to find Ron's body?"

"I don't know, Sam. You tell me."

She waved the glowing screen

of her phone around. "Got it!"

Sam began tapping the keypad. "Er… wait a second… no, not that one, here we go. Old Widow Hoggins has a

# THE CRAWLING HAND

warehouse under the railway arches on Church Lane."

"And?" I said.

"Here's what I found. There was only one delivery there. It was late last night, just at the same time that Ron woke up to find himself without his body."

"So what shall we do – grab the skeletons and march them back home?"

"No. Something much more scary. It's time we paid Widow Hoggins a little visit!"

# THE CRAWLING HAND

## CHAPTER 4

The door under the railway arches was locked tight. "What now?" I whispered.

The hand spoke up. "Leave this to me. Sam, please hold me next to the keyhole."

Sam did as she was told. The hand stuck its middle finger into the hole. Two seconds later, there was a click.

"Wow! How did you do that?" I was impressed.

# THE CRAWLING HAND

"Have you never heard of a skeleton key?" the hand replied.

"Ha!" said Sam. "Dead funny!"

The door swung open. The darkness behind it was filled with a strange shuffling sound.

"Erm. What if there's burglars in there?"

"It's not burglars you should be scared of Jas. Remember, we are looking for loads of dead people, right?"

"Yeah. I was trying not to think of that."

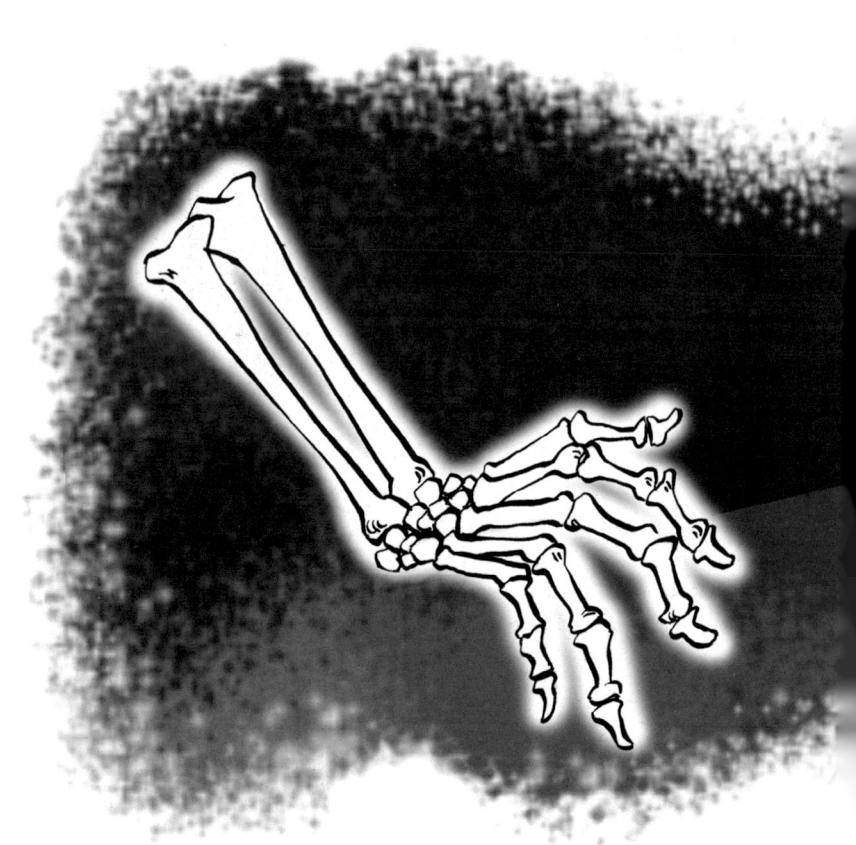

# The Crawling Hand

The hand leaped like a spider onto the ground. A moment later a light came on. In the middle of the empty room, there was a huge packing case.

"Master!" the hand cried. "I'm coming." Quick as a flash, the hand moved over the floor and onto the case. Sharp finger bones sliced away the plastic cover. "Help me, please!"

Sam and Jas ran over and grabbed the lid.

"I'm not ready for this!" I muttered.

# THE CRAWLING HAND

"Too late to go back now!" I grunted, lifting the lid. There was the evidence. Right before our eyes. A jumble of bones suddenly jigging about, turning back into skeletons.

The hand hopped up and down like a puppy.

"Master! Master!"

One of the skeletons bent over and gently picked up the hand. "My faithful servant!" it murmured as it stuck the hand back on.

Then it turned and stared at the two of us. All his skinny friends began walking towards us.

"We're so dead!" I said.

# THE CRAWLING HAND

## CHAPTER 5

"No Son, it's not you that's dead, but us!" One of the skeletons laughed. "Thank you for saving us!" He held out a hand. I had no choice but to shake the cold bones.

"Poor things" said Sam.

Then she smiled wickedly. "I hope you're in the mood for revenge!"

The skeletons gave the thumbs up.

"Just follow me," said Sam.

"Do you know where we're going?" I hissed as we ran down the street.

"Yes!" Sam replied. "Lucky that Widow Hoggins lives round here!"

It was also lucky no one was

# THE CRAWLING HAND

around. What would they have thought of two kids and a gang of skeletons out jogging?

The front door was easy, thanks to Ron's finger. We let the skeletons go ahead of us. They burst into the bedroom. It was Ron who warned

Widow Hoggins not to scream. She was shaking in her bed. "But I thought you were…."

"Dead. Yes. And I was sleeping soundly before your diggers woke me up. Now how about you find us all nice new coffins and take the building site away unless…"

# THE CRAWLING HAND

"Unless what?" she sobbed.

"You wish to be haunted for the rest of your days!" said Ron.

And so that was that then. Thanks to my amazing skills, the case was solved. Yes, I suppose Sam helped a bit. There's a lovely park on the building site these days. Ron and his mates are having a good long rest and Widow Hoggins has a lot more locks on her doors!

# FOR TEACHERS

## About Freestylers

Freestylers is a series of carefully levelled stories, especially geared for struggling readers of both sexes. With very low reading age and high interest age, these books are humorous, fun, up-to-the-minute and edgy. Core characters provide familiarity in all of the stories, build confidence and ease pupils from one story through to the next, accelerating reading progress.

Freestylers can be used for both guided and independent reading. To make the most of the books you can:

• Focus on making each reading session successful. Talk about the text before the pupil starts reading. Introduce the characters, the storyline and any unfamiliar vocabulary.

• Encourage the pupil to talk about the book during reading and after reading. How would they have felt if they were Jas? Or Sam? How would they have gone about solving the mystery?

• Talk about which parts of the story they like best and why.

**For guidance, this story has been approximately measured to:**

National Curriculum Level: 3C
Reading Age: 7
Book Band: Lime

ATOS: 2.6
Lexile ® Measure [confirmed]: 360L